TRUCKER'S
Night Before Christmas

TRUCKER'S Night Before Christmas

Written by David Davis
Illustrated by James Rice

PELICAN PUBLISHING COMPANY
Gretna 1999

*For my two dads, A. D. Davis and George Chiappini, and also for
Mrs. Cathy Brown, my long-suffering high school journalism teacher*

*The word "Pelican" and the depiction of a pelican are trademarks
of Pelican Publishing Company, Inc., and are registered
in the U.S. Patent and Trademark Office.*

Library of Congress Cataloging-in-Publication Data

Davis, David (David R.), 1948 -
   Trucker's night before Christmas / written by David Davis ;
illustrated by James Rice
   p. cm.
   SUMMARY: In this parody of the famous poem by Clement C. Moore,
Santa Claus is a trucker in a red jumpsuit and cap who pays a visit
to those at the Midway truck stop on Christmas Eve.
   ISBN 1-56554-656-3
   1. Christmas Juvenile poetry. 2. Truck drivers Juvenile poetry.
3. Santa Claus Juvenile poetry. 4. Children's poetry, American. [1.
Santa Claus Poetry. 2. Christmas Poetry. 3. Truck drivers Poetry.
4. American poetry. 5. Narrative poetry.] I. Rice, James, 1934 -
ill. II. Title.
   PS3554.A93344 T78 1999

                                                        99-30580
                                                           CIP

Mack, Kenworth, Peterbuilt, Chevy, Ford, and No-Doze are registered trademarks.

Printed in Korea

Published by Pelican Publishing Company, Inc.
1000 Burmaster Street, Gretna, Louisiana 70053

Trucker's Night Before Christmas

'Long a cold Christmas highway at the Midway truck stop
The rig jockeys were weary, they just had to flop.
The waitress hung orders on the old kitchen wall,
She yelled, "Burgers, undressed! Side orders for all!"

Outside the café on the cold concrete lot,
The rigs were lined up, each one in it's spot.
The engines on idle out there on the slab,
Made a warm place to sleep for some guys in their cabs.

I missed all my kinfolk on this Christmas Eve,
Gave a hitchhiker a ride so he wouldn't freeze.
I tore up two retreads a ways up the line,
So I paid the mechanic for two that were fine.

I turned on my stool and looked over the place,
And read the holiday thoughts on each driver's face.
They had to be haulin' their loads all alone,
While other folks opened their presents at home.

Truckers phoned their dispatchers, then parked in their booths,
They filled out their logbooks (and some wrote the truth).
The waitress poured coffee and I laid down my tip,
We talked of the weather—and I flirted a bit.

When out on the lot there commenced such a roar.
A huge diesel engine revved outside the door!
Away to the window I flew in one jump,
Thought a semi had jackknifed and rammed the gas pump!

The glow of the sign that said "Stop, Fuel, and Eat,"
Flashed on and off on the wet asphalt street.
A red, speeding Mack truck sure looked like cop bait,
With that many presents—his load's overweight!

With the little old driver, I hoped we had luck,
It must be St. Nick and his swank Christmas truck.
His headlights were blazin', his runnin' lights seen,
All different bright shades of red, white, and green.

We all heard him singin' as he jumped out the cab,
His feet hit the ground 'fore his brakes started to grab!
"I've driven a Kenworth, and a Peterbuilt, too!
A Mack, Chevy, and a Ford, a-haulin' for you!"

"I'm drivin'! All loaded!
Now, engine and air brakes!
High Ballin'!" He shouted,
"Through 'smokies' and snowflakes!

To the front of the pumps,
To the café's front wall!
This old Christmas-time trucker,
Is a real ratchet jaw!"

As fast rigs in a convoy down the night highway fly,
When they have a straight roadway, and no radar eye.
So up to the hash house the Yule driver flew,
With a truckload of gifts, and a new air horn, too.

And then in a minute, I heard by the door
The sound of his steel-toes on the old café floor.
I spilled all my java, rubberneckin' around,
With the Christmas-time trucker near my spot on the ground.

He had on a jumpsuit that was fire-engine red,
To match the red cap that he had on his head.
A bundle of gifts he had on his back,
And he smiled at me as he opened the sack.

His eyes—how they twinkled! His laughter, how merry!!
(Like when you find some cheap diesel, and get all you can carry!)
This Christmas-time trucker was a real midnight flyer,
And his beard was as white as a new whitewall tire!

He asked for a thermos of coffee straight black,
And a fill-up of fuel tanks to carry him back.
He had a broad face and a junk-food type body,
There was loot for us all. (And that ain't too shoddy!)

He gave Velma, the waitress, track shoes and some socks,
And a bottle of color for her homemade blonde locks.
He tossed me a billfold attached to a chain,
And a radar detector for my driving pain.

He didn't talk much 'cause he couldn't stay,
Wheeled in a new jukebox with music to play.
He gave us all coupons for chicken-fried steaks.
And goose-feather vests so we could foil the shakes.

He gave sleepy ol' Hiram a box of No-Doze,
And some snazzy sunglasses went to a driver named Rose.

He'd paid off some tickets for a feller named Boggs,
And gave him a job lead, so he could quit haulin' hogs.

Nick tipped all the workers a brand new, crisp twenty,
And said, "Got to go—I got truck stops a plenty!
If I don't keep to my schedule, I'll be in a fix!
Time to get on the road, and start wigglin' that stick!"

He cranked up his rig, and we all heard him say,
"I'll miss the weigh stations—I'll take the back way!"

Nick boomed on the CB as he hauled off his load,
"Merry Christmas truck jockeys, see y'all down the road!"